Tom's Clockwork Dragon

For Dad — J.E.
For Gerry — M.O.

OXFORD
UNIVERSITY PRESS

Great Clarendon Street, Oxford OX2 6DP

Oxford University Press is a department of the University of Oxford.
It furthers the University's objective of excellence in research, scholarship,
and education by publishing worldwide in

Oxford New York
Auckland Cape Town Dar es Salaam Hong Kong Karachi
Kuala Lumpur Madrid Melbourne Mexico City Nairobi
New Delhi Shanghai Taipei Toronto

With offices in
Argentina Austria Brazil Chile Czech Republic France Greece
Guatemala Hungary Italy Japan Poland Portugal Singapore
South Korea Switzerland Thailand Turkey Ukraine Vietnam

Oxford is a registered trade mark of Oxford University Press
in the UK and in certain other countries

British Library Cataloguing in Publication Data available

ISBN: 978-0-19-276335-8 (Hardback)
ISBN: 978-0-19-276336-5 (Paperback)

10 9 8 7 6 5 4 3 2 1

You can find out more about Jonathan Emmett's books by
visiting his website at www.scribblestreet.co.uk

You can find out more about Mark Oliver by visiting his
website at www.olly.net

Printed in China

Tom's Clockwork Dragon

Jonathan Emmett & Mark Oliver

OXFORD
UNIVERSITY PRESS

'Finished!' said Tom. He wound up the little clockwork horse and watched it gallop across the workbench.

Just then Tom's master, the Toymaker, returned. *Crash!* The horse galloped off the edge of the bench and smashed to pieces on the floor.

'What was that?' scowled the Toymaker, who had spent the whole day at market without selling a single toy.

'It *was* a clockwork horse,' sighed Tom, gathering up the pieces.

'I've told you, cogs and springs are for *clocks* – not toys,' snapped the Toymaker. 'You were supposed to be painting puppets not wasting *another* day on your ridiculous *clockwork!* You're a useless apprentice and YOU'RE FIRED!' he shouted, as he threw Tom out of the door.

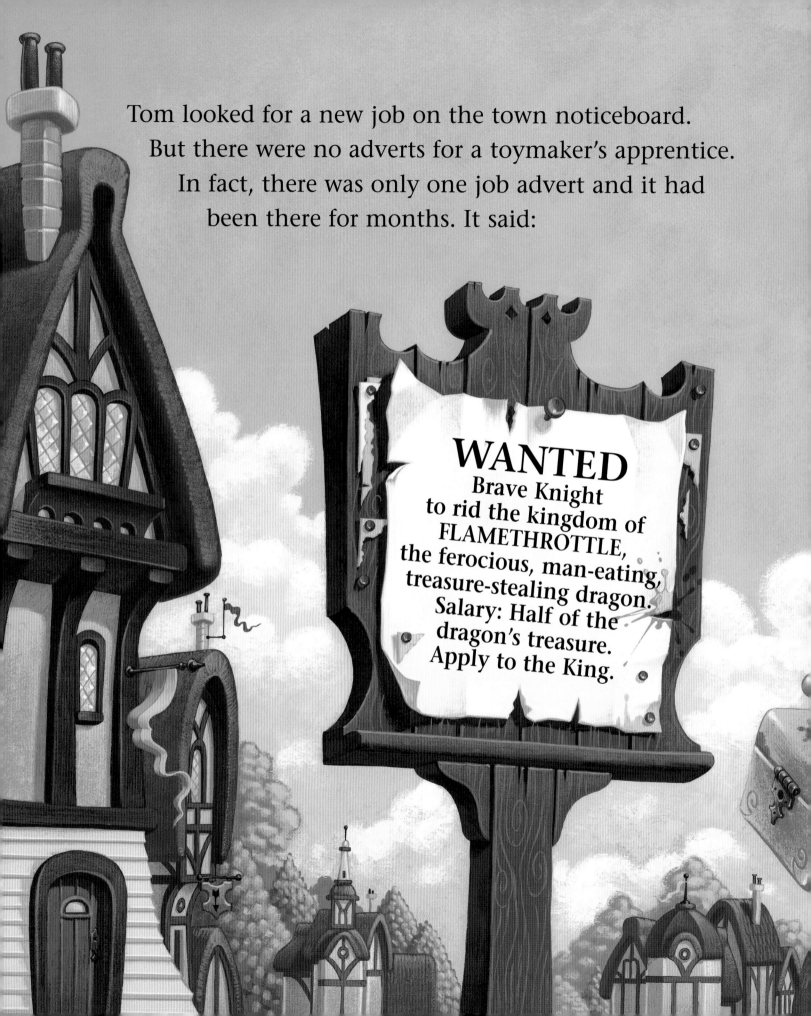

Tom looked for a new job on the town noticeboard.
But there were no adverts for a toymaker's apprentice.
In fact, there was only one job advert and it had
been there for months. It said:

WANTED
Brave Knight
to rid the kingdom of
FLAMETHROTTLE,
the ferocious, man-eating,
treasure-stealing dragon.
Salary: Half of the
dragon's treasure.
Apply to the King.

'Well,' thought Tom,
'it's the only job there is,
so I suppose I should
give it a try.'

The King nearly fell off his throne laughing when Tom turned up at the palace. 'The advert was for a *brave knight* not a *foolish boy*,' he said, wiping his eyes. 'But since all the real knights have been eaten by the dragon, I suppose you might as well try. But you need to be properly dressed,' he added. 'Go and ask the armourer to knock up a suit in your size.'

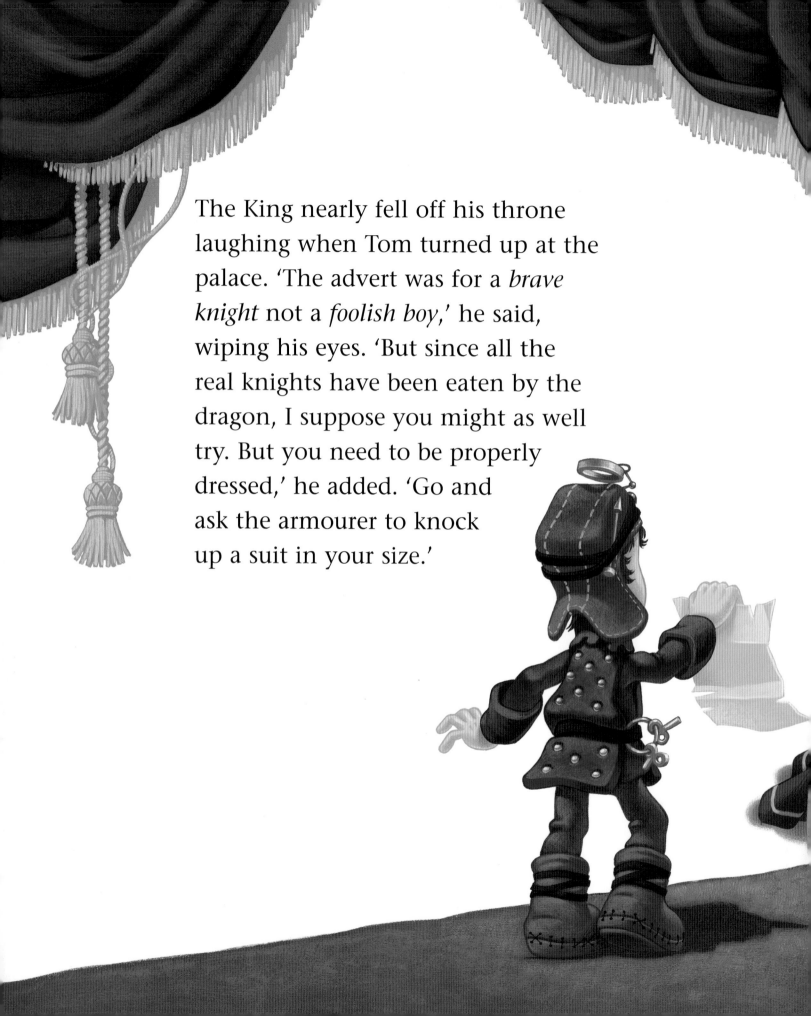

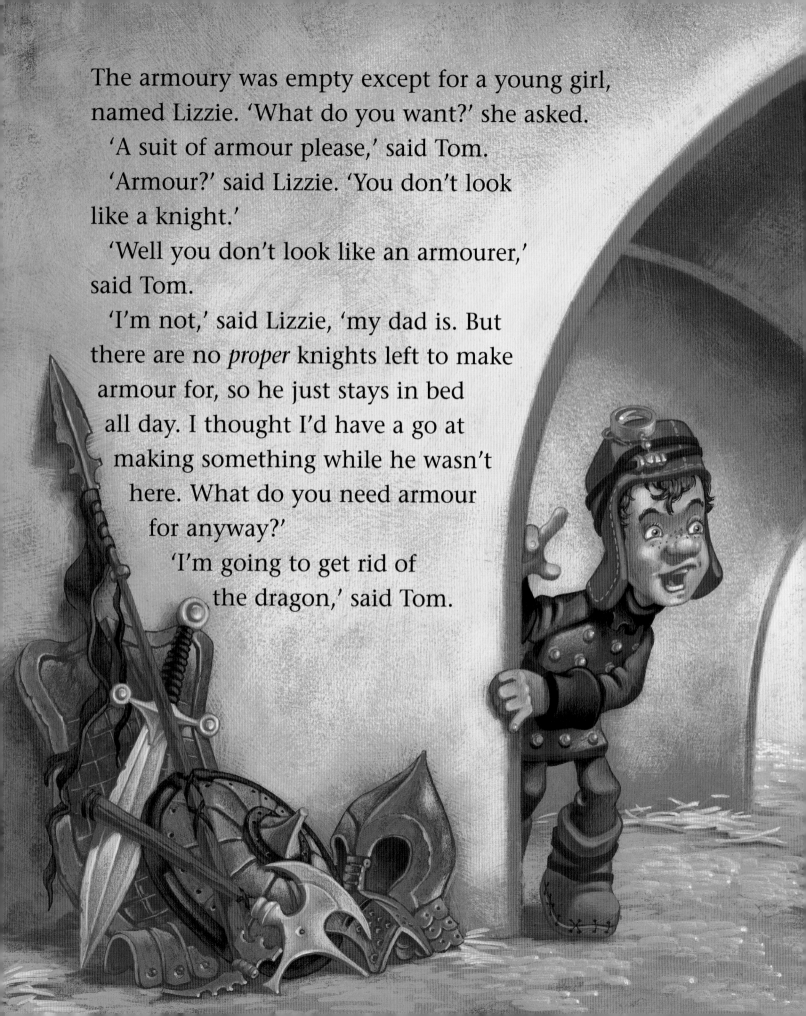

The armoury was empty except for a young girl, named Lizzie. 'What do you want?' she asked.

'A suit of armour please,' said Tom.

'Armour?' said Lizzie. 'You don't look like a knight.'

'Well you don't look like an armourer,' said Tom.

'I'm not,' said Lizzie, 'my dad is. But there are no *proper* knights left to make armour for, so he just stays in bed all day. I thought I'd have a go at making something while he wasn't here. What do you need armour for anyway?'

'I'm going to get rid of the dragon,' said Tom.

Lizzie laughed. 'You? You'll never do it. The only thing that would drive that dragon away is a bigger, scarier dragon.'

But Lizzie's words had given Tom an idea. '*Drive* it away,' he repeated slowly to himself. 'I think I know what to do,' he said, 'but I'm going to need your help!'

Later that night, Tom and Lizzie crept to the cave where Flamethrottle lay asleep. The dragon was twice the size that Tom had expected and three times as scary-looking.

'I'm not sure that this is a good idea,' said Tom, weakly.

'Don't be silly,' whispered Lizzie. 'You said you needed lots of scrap metal, and there's heaps of it here.'

And she was right. The mouth of the cave was littered with armour, which was all that was left of the brave knights who had dared to go inside.

'Come on,' hissed Lizzie. And they began to gather up the armour as quietly as they could.

Back at the workshop, Tom
and Lizzie took all the armour
to pieces and began to make
something new.

They worked for seven days . . .

and seven nights . . .

heating . . .

and hammering . . .

pumping the bellows . . .

and stoking
the fire,
until . . .

'It's finished!' said Lizzie, fastening
the last plate in place.
'It's MAGNIFICENT,' said Tom
admiring their creation.
'It had better work!' yawned Lizzie.
'Of course it will work,' said Tom,
picking up an enormous key. 'Just as
soon as I've wound it up.'

Flamethrottle was woken the next
morning by a loud clanking sound.

He charged out to have whoever it was for breakfast, but found a bigger, fiercer-looking dragon waiting outside.

'WHAT ARE YOU DOING HERE?' demanded the new dragon in a harsh metallic voice.

'Er . . . I live here,' said Flamethrottle weakly.

'NOT ANY MORE YOU DON'T,' bellowed the giant dragon. 'OUT!'

'R-r-right,' stuttered Flamethrottle, glancing back at the treasure. 'P-p-perhaps I could just collect a few . . .'

'OUT NOW!' roared the giant dragon, chasing the terrified Flamethrottle away from the cave.

'I told you this would work!' grinned Tom, as he pulled on the controls of the clockwork dragon.

'It's not over yet,' said Lizzie, as they crashed out of a forest and leapt over a startled cow.

They had almost chased Flamethrottle right out of the kingdom, when the huge mechanical legs slowed down and then ground to a halt. Tom fiddled frantically with the controls, but nothing happened.

'The clockwork motor must have run down,' he groaned.

Flamethrottle noticed that he was no longer being chased and crept back cautiously to investigate.

'Is something wrong?' he asked, from a safe distance.

'Er . . . no . . . everything's fine,' said Tom, speaking through the metal horn that made the clockwork dragon's voice. 'I'm just having a rest.'

But Flamethrottle didn't believe him. There was something odd about this giant dragon – its skin was too shiny and it moved in a strange way.

Tom and Lizzie were getting desperate. 'If he breathes fire on us, we'll be baked alive,' whispered Lizzie. 'If only we could wind up the motor,' said Tom.

Meanwhile, Flamethrottle had circled closer to inspect the dragon.

'What's that big key for?' he asked.

Then Tom had another of his ideas. 'PLEASE don't touch that!' he called. 'It's very important.'

'What did you tell him that for?' hissed Lizzie.

'Why is it important?'
demanded Flamethrottle.
'Because I'm a mechanical
dragon,' replied Tom, 'and if
you turn that key, my *legs will
lock* and I won't be able to
chase after you.'
'Really?' said
Flamethrottle gleefully,
and he grabbed the key
and gave it a turn.
Tom heaved a sigh of relief.
His idea was working.

'*Please* don't turn it again,' wailed Tom. 'If you do, my *claws will lock* and I won't be able to grab you.'

And Flamethrottle, thinking he had got the better of the giant dragon, couldn't resist giving the key another couple of turns.

'*Please* stop,' whimpered Tom once more, 'or my *jaws will lock* and I won't be able to chomp you up.'

So of course, Flamethrottle seized the key and turned it again and again until it would turn no more.

'Now I've got you!' yelled Flamethrottle triumphantly.

'No, now I've got *you!*' said Tom, pulling hard on the controls.

The fully-wound
clockwork dragon
sprang up and
lurched forwards
with gaping jaws.

'YAARGHHH!' screamed Flamethrottle,
as the razor-sharp teeth snapped shut
a hair's breadth from his snout.
And – without stopping to
see if the metal dragon's legs
and claws were also working –
he scrambled off and out of
the kingdom and was never
seen again.

The King was pleased to be rid of the *real* dragon and *delighted* when Tom and Lizzie presented him with the *clockwork* dragon as well. It made a wonderful royal carriage for parades. In return, the King gave Tom and Lizzie half of Flamethrottle's treasure as promised.

They used the reward to set up a
clockwork toyshop, where they
made and sold the most
wonderful clockwork toys.
The shop sold everything from
clockwork archers to clockwork zebras,
but their most popular toy was –
well, can you guess?

Yes, it was their *little*
clockwork dragons, of course.